Lil' Black Girl from the Beach:

A Wake-Up Call from God

N. Hemingway

1

Table of Contents

Prologue: A Wake-Up Call!

"Dang, I need to stop smoking reefer!" I thought to myself as I took a sip of water. Wayne and I had just finished making love, and it was the best ever! Multiple orgasms, and Wayne and I were laughing and having a great time during our love making. It was pure bliss! After I placed the glass back on the night table, I turned over and glanced at Wayne's alarm clock and noted the time of 11:54 pm. Then I started getting a strong sense of déjà vu. The clock struck 11:55 pm, and something clicked in my mind that I was getting ready to die. And I felt a sharp pain in my chest.

"Wayne! Call 9-1-1! I think I'm having a heart attack!" I yelled out while I clutched my chest. Wayne came running out of the bathroom, and before he could pick up the phone, I said to him, "Wayne, the phone won't work." He picked up the phone anyway, and there was no dial tone—the phone was dead. He came running over to my side of the bed to get my cell phone, and before he got there, I said, "Wayne, you can't find my phone." And sure enough, my cell wasn't on my night table. I *always* plug my phone up and place it on my night table before I go to bed. Wayne started looking through my purse, but no luck, so he left to go to the African-themed guest room to get that phone.

I panicked and left the bedroom, heading to the first floor. "What are you doing Neesy!" Wayne shouted at me as he tried to catch me running down the stairs. He caught up to me as I was trying to open the front door. But he kept me inside the house and navigated me to the dining room. There I started "beating" on him–patting his face and head while telling him I loved him over and over. I closed my eyes and continued feeling on Wayne's face, head, and upper body. I was trying to memorize Wayne and commit his features to memory.

"Cee Cee! Cee Cee! Call 9-1-1!" Wayne yelled to our daughter. Cee Cee was on the stairs with the phone in her hands crying. She was upset to see her mom in such bad shape. Wayne got me to lie down on the floor in the dining room and talked to the 9-1-1 operator on the phone. But I knew I wasn't going to make it before the ambulance arrived. I motioned for Cee Cee to come to me because speech had become exceedingly difficult at that time. Cee Cee brought me a glass of water, and I started talking to my sweetie. We reminisced about some of her childhood events, like dance and gymnastics. I also told her to stick to her books and that boys weren't about nothing but getting into her panties. Then this amazing thing happened. I caught a glimpse of Cee Cee's future— that she would be a beautiful bride, what type of career her husband would have, and how many children she would have. I was getting ready to see Wayne's future when my mind went blank!

"You're going to be ok. Everything is going to be alright," I heard a voice tell me. Wayne swore that I was gone when I heard that voice. Before my mind went blank, I felt my body starting to shut down and that my time was running out. I even felt organs in my body start to shut down—kidneys, liver, lungs—with my heart waiting to be the last to go. The sharp pain was still there. I was going to die on my dining room floor naked—not a pretty way to go!

"Your eyes just popped open, you stood straight up, and you told me you felt fine," Wayne later told me. I then fell straight back into his arms and started to convulse but without any of the eye rolling or my tongue coming out of my mouth. By this time a police officer arrived but didn't help Wayne with me. I convulsed for a few minutes as Wayne called my name. Once I stopped, I heard Wayne asking me what my name was, and I answered, "Neesy." Then the police officer asked me a series of questions about where I was, who Wayne was, etc. The paramedics arrived and did a piss poor exam (pulse only) and offered to take me to the hospital. I declined more from being naked under a comforter than anything else. I also believed that as sure as my name is Danice, any EKG would reveal that I did not suffer a heart attack!

* * *

"Commander Harris, I'll fax this letter to your supervisor requesting that you have the next four weeks off immediately," Dr. Carter, my shrink, told me over the phone. "I'll prescribe some valium for you, and I'll see you tomorrow at 2 pm." I confirmed the session and thanked her for giving me some time off. Then I hung up the phone and laid back down in the bed to cry. I had been doing that for the last few days because my nerves were so rattled by almost dying.

You got to stop crying, Neesy! I berated myself for the thousandth time. I'd just been lying in bed for the last three weeks, crying off and on and asking God what I should do and why didn't I die. Of course, I didn't get an answer! Wayne and Cee Cee would call and check on me throughout the day. Sometimes I answered and other times I didn't because I was crying. I would try to put on a cheerful tone, but I knew Wayne was worried. I also convinced him that we still needed to take our planned trip to South Carolina so that Cee Cee and one of her friends could attend the Clemson University Tigers football game. Since she was in high school, we wanted her to experience some of college life, like taking college classes on a college campus and tailgating before a college football game.

* * *

"This car drives like a dream!" I told Wayne as we cruised on I-85 south heading to South Carolina. I had bought my dream car—a BMW—a couple of months ago, and this was our first road trip since the purchase. I decided on the X-5 over the 5 series, because we would have more room for luggage and could fold down the seats if someone wanted to lie down during long trips. "I have to give it to BMW. They make a smooth ride!" Wayne replied as he navigated the car on the highway. Cee Cee had invited her friend Monique, another cheerleader from her high school squad, to go to Clemson with us. I was cool with Monique coming because I had known her mom, Jackie, for a few years since she had been my personal trainer for a while.

"We're here!" Cee Cee and Monique exclaimed as we passed the "Welcome to Tiger Country" sign and neared our hotel in Clemson. I was glad that we were early enough to check into our rooms, relax, and then get something to eat. We had brought a cooler full of food and a mini grill to cook on at the tailgate the next day. Some friends of ours from Myrtle Beach were coming up for the game as well, so we were going to have a good time eating, drinking, and getting pumped up before the game!

* * *

"Daddy and Mommy, thank you for bringing me and Monique to Clemson," Cee Cee told me and Wayne.

"Yes! Thank you so much Mr. and Mrs. Harris for allowing me to come. I had a great time!" Monique gushed from the back seat. We were in the post-game bumper-to-bumper traffic trying to get back to the hotel. I was glad that the game was at 1 pm so we could get a good night's sleep before heading out early Sunday morning. We had adjoining rooms so the girls could have their privacy, but we could check on them during the night. Little did I know that Someone would be checking on me during the night!

"Get up Neesy!" I heard a voice calling me. "Get up Neesy!" I heard the voice again, and I immediately sat up in the bed. Looking around the room, I saw no one, but I still felt a presence. I quickly got out of bed, went to the foot of the bed, and got on my knees. "God, I'm so sorry for what I've done! I'm sorry for the reefer smoking, cussing, adultery, and talking about people," I sobbed with snot running down my face mixing with the tears. "Lord, forgive me for all the sins I've committed, and I welcome you, Jesus, into my heart!" I confessed in a trembling voice. Here I was, in a hotel room at 2 am, crying and snot running, and Wayne is in the bed out cold! I guess that's how God wanted it to be. On October 25th, exactly a month after my near-death experience, I gave my life to Jesus Christ as my personal Lord and Savior.

Now, I'm going to take you on a journey on how I came to this place of forgiveness and repentance!

Chapter 1: How I Get By!

"Rich!" I cried out as I felt the sensation building. I waited a few minutes, then I shouted out again, "Rich!"

I heard some movement, then his sleepy voice mumbling, "I'm coming," from across the hall. Rich came in and lifted me out of the top bunk that I shared with my sister, Rhonda, and took me to the bathroom. I was five years old and wore braces on my legs, so going to the bathroom at night could be a chore.

I wore the braces at night to help straighten my legs because I was severely knock-kneed, and the doctor told my mom that wearing them would straighten my legs and knees. Otherwise, he would go back to the original plan of breaking my legs and resetting them. My mom declined that option, so I had been a leg-braces-wearing child for the last two years. In order to get to the bathroom, I had to master the art of maneuvering out of bed, climbing down from the top bunk, then hopping about twenty feet to the bathroom.

I usually slept on the top bunk because the other sisters didn't want to sleep with Rhonda because she talked in her sleep.

Plus, I was an equal opportunity sleeper- I went from room to room and slept with anyone in the house who would let me in their bed! Oftentimes than not, I would leave a trail of pee behind me because I couldn't make it to the bathroom in time. This trip to the bathroom was a success because my big brother Rich was in town, so I had no problem getting relief in time.

"Look at Alice," one of the girls at school whispered while pointing. We all turned to look at Alice who was painfully walking around the playground with the help of one of the teacher's aides. Alice wore braces on her legs, but hers were on individual legs, whereas mine had bars connecting the braces together. Alice didn't have many friends because she couldn't run and jump like the rest of us five-year-olds. I said a silent prayer, thanking God that I didn't have to wear my braces out in public like Alice.

During the era of the mid-1970s when I grew up, your popularity as a five-year-old would be shot if you had something that was so different from your peers. Any kind of "defect" or "abnormality" kept you isolated or shunned by the "normal" kids. You weren't invited to play kickball, tag, or jump rope. And you could forget about going to any birthday parties or sleepovers because you didn't fit in. I didn't envy Alice but was glad that my "defect" wasn't seen by all.

* * *

"We're going to the Philippines!" we all shouted after my mother delivered the news that we were moving there because it was my dad's next duty station. This would to be my first move as an Air Force brat since I had only lived in my hometown of Myrtle Beach, SC, all of my life. Excitement built in me as I imagined my first plane ride to a place I had never dreamed of or even heard about. Over the next few months, we got our belongings together to make the big move to a new country.

It was finally time to leave, and my sister, Rhonda, jumped up ready to go with us until Big Momma told her to sit her butt down because she wasn't going nowhere. That was the moment Rhonda realized that Renee, my mom, wasn't her mom, too. Renee was actually her oldest sister but had done much of her caregiving because Big Momma and Big Daddy worked a lot. As Rhonda sat there crying, me, my younger brother Terry, and my mom said our goodbyes to the rest of the family.

* * *

"Make it stop!" I cried to my mom as I kept my hands over my ears with tears rolling down my cheeks. The excitement I felt on the plane quickly vanished when we ascended higher into the sky and my ears began to hurt terribly. I had a mouth full of gum and was chewing furiously, but I got no relief from the pressure in my ears. A flight attendant came by to check on me and to tell me that my ears should pop soon, and then I could enjoy the rest of my flight. My ears never popped, so I was a miserable, gum-chewing child for the rest of the trip.

* * *

"Mom, can I have that doll?" I eagerly asked as I eyed the beautiful doll in the gift shop. The doll I wanted was a Hawaiian hula girl that had a lei on her head, and she was dressed in a grass skirt with coconut shells covering her breasts. The three of us were in Hawaii for a layover before our trip to the Philippines resumed.

My mom looked at me and said, "No. What did I tell y'all when we're in a store? 'Don't look at nothing. Don't touch nothing, and don't ask for nothing because you ain't getting nothing,'" I knew this reply by rote because my mom had drilled this saying into the heads of me and my brother for years. My mom was a typical Black mother. We wouldn't dare step out of line in a store—the look my mom would give us was enough to keep us silent and in line. I looked at the $5 doll with longing, but knew she was going to stay on that shelf. My brother and I occupied ourselves by reading comic books during our long layover at Hickam Air Force Base in Honolulu, Hawaii.

"Wow! This place is beautiful!" my brother Terry exclaimed as our dad was driving us through the streets of Luzon, Philippines to our home. The sky was so blue, with fluffy white clouds drifting along. There were so many coconut trees with coconuts hanging underneath them. Terry and I were fascinated because we had never seen a coconut tree. We were also in awe because there were so many people on the streets, and they didn't look like us. My dad told us that the people are Filipinos, and that we were strangers in their country. Terry and I looked on in fascination as we saw people with cone-shaped hats on their heads riding bicycles, and people walking the streets with fruit baskets and other strange things on their heads. Our heads were swiveling from left to right trying to soak in this new culture we were thrust into.

"We're home," my dad announced as he pulled the car into the driveway of our house. Terry and I stood bug-eyed as we looked at the two-story stucco-like house with coconut trees in the yard. We had never lived in a two-story home, so having stairs to go up and down on and a banister to slide on was going to be fun!

"Take off your shoes," my dad commanded as we entered the house. Mom, Terry, and I looked at my dad like he had grown five heads, because we always wore shoes in the house. My dad said, "This is what the Filipinos do, and I've come to like their custom." My mom, my brother, and I shrugged our shoulders and proceeded to take off our shoes at the front door and line them up with my dad's shoes that were already neatly placed there. Once that was done, my brother and I tore through the house exploring the place we would call home for the next two and a half years.

"There are bedrooms downstairs!" yelled my brother Terry to our parents.

"And there are two bedrooms up here!" I yelled from the upstairs landing.

"We're gonna have our own rooms!" Terry and I yelled at the same time. But my mom dashed those dreams quickly as she said, "I'm not having my babies sleep downstairs. Y'all will be sharing the room upstairs across the hall from me and your daddy." Terry and I groaned as we realized that we would be sharing a room, but it was good that we didn't have to share a bed like we did at the house of Big Momma and Big Daddy.

Once we unpacked our suitcases, we went back downstairs to eat lunch. Terry and I thought we were going to eat at the big table, but Dad told us that the kids' table was right there under the staircase. In most families during my childhood, the grown-ups ate at the big table, and the kids ate at the kids' table until they got to be teenagers. Then they graduated to the big table. My brother and I ate at the big table on special occasions like Thanksgiving, Christmas, and New Year's Day. My brother and I even had our own "special" cups that we drank out of—mine was red, and his was blue. That way there was no arguing over who had whose cup. My mom was smart that way because she knew how kids could argue over the most insignificant things, having helped to raise seven of her eight siblings.

We quickly settled into our routine of living in a new country, house, and neighborhood. Going to a new school was scary since I had only been to school for half the year in my hometown. I was friendly, but I was shy, and the other children in the class had to approach me first and ask me to play with them. This shyness followed me into adulthood. "You have a pretty smile for a Black girl," one of my teachers told me.

"Thank you," I replied back as I was taught to do if someone gave me a compliment. This wasn't the first time I had heard that I had a pretty smile for a Black girl—my two kindergarten teachers back home said that to me, along with other adults in the community. I would find out years later that I had a pretty smile for a dark-skinned girl. Yes, racism and colorism existed within my own race. As a child I'm looking at this from the Black-White perspective, but in reality, it was a Black-Black perspective where skin color *did* matter. I'll pick this topic back up later.

Chapter 2: So the Nightmare Begins . . .

My parents were going out for a night of dancing at the NCO Club, so that meant Terry and I needed a babysitter. We had a live-in nanny, but she went home on the weekends to be with her family. We also had a yard boy who cut the grass and maintained the yard and a sewing woman who sewed our clothes. Why we had a sewing woman when my mom could sew her butt off was crazy to me. We were living like Black royalty with all the people who worked for my parents. My brother and I didn't know that Filipino workers were cheap, so even a Senior Airman (E-4) like my dad could afford to live large overseas. My mom interviewed a couple of the teenaged girls in the neighborhood and decided on fourteen-year-old Fortuna. Fortuna's name means "good fortune" in Filipino, but for Terry and me she was a bad fortune that stayed with us for two years.

"Come here Danice," Fortuna called to me in her accented English. I slowly approached her where she was sitting on my bed. Once I got there, she pulled me onto the bed with her, then pulled the sheet over us. She violated my five-year-old body by kissing me and touching me in places no one should have. After she was done with me, Fortuna lifted up the sheet and allowed me to leave the bed. I walked over to the bed where my three-year-old brother Terry sat. She next called him over to her, and his violation began. I sat on my brother's twin bed in a daze, trying to process what had just happened to me. When she had finished with my brother, he joined me on his bed looking as dazed as I was. Once Fortuna put on her clothes, she told Terry and me not to say anything to our parents. Being the good and polite Southern children we were raised to be, we both replied, "Yes ma'am." This nightmare of frequent molestations of me and my brother lasted for two years.

* * *

"Danice, you are too old to be peeing in the bed," my mom stated once she discovered my wet bed. All I could do was look at her with shameful eyes because I didn't have an answer for her. It had been a few months since Fortuna had started molesting Terry and me, and I had started peeing the bed a couple of weeks ago. This wetting the bed continued until I entered high school. I didn't find out until I was grown and married that my peeing the bed was stimulated by being molested as a child. The horrors Terry and I endured at the hands of Fortuna were something I wanted to forget, so I pushed down and suppressed those memories for thirty years.

* * *

"Astrid, look at my leg!" I cried as I ran into the house. Blood was running down my leg from a dog bite I had just gotten from a neighbor's loose dog.

"What happened to you?" Astrid asked as she examined my leg. I told her how I was walking to the school bus stop when this dog came out of nowhere and ran up to me barking and growling. Next thing I knew, the dog ran up on me and bit my leg, then ran off toward some houses. I didn't cry as our nanny, Astrid, treated my leg. After she was done patching me up, Astrid called a cab to take me to school since I had missed the bus. This was my first cab ride, and I was excited, hoping that my friends would see me pulling up to school in a cab instead of the regular old school bus. Being in the first grade now, I felt like a real big kid riding in the taxi. I showed off my band-aid to friends and told them how the dog bit me and how I wasn't afraid of the dog.

Once my parents got home later that day, Astrid and I told them about the dog biting incident, and they went out and talked to some neighbors to locate the dog. The dog was located, and my parents found out that the dog had current vaccinations, so I didn't have to go through the ordeal of getting multiple rabies shots. I had an exciting day for a six-year-old. First, I was bitten by a dog, then I rode in a cab. Could my life have gotten any more exciting? We'll see . . .

Chapter 3: Four Years Later

. . .

"Do y'all want to change your last names from Adams to Johnson?" my mom asked me and my brother.

"No! We like Adams better," Terry and I chorused at the same time. I had just turned ten, and it was time for me to have my own military ID card. We had lived on Altus AFB in Altus, Oklahoma, for the last two years, so I knew this day was coming. My mom took me to the place to get my military ID, and that's when I found out that Terry and my last name had been changed to Johnson. I felt anger at my mom for not telling us of the name change, but what could I do since she was the adult?

She shouldn't have even asked us if she wasn't going to listen to us, I thought to myself as we waited for me to get my ID card. Afterward, we went to the Shopette where I made my first purchase using my ID card. It was exciting because I had just crossed a much-anticipated rite of passage as a military brat—I had received the exalted military ID card.

* * *

The look in the store clerks' eyes showed how I felt when I placed the box of Kotex pads on the counter. Both of the women showed embarrassment, which was exactly how I felt because at twelve years old, I was in the Shopette purchasing my own sanitary products. My mom thought nothing was wrong with sending her twelve-year-old daughter to the store to buy her own pads. But I felt embarrassment and shame every time I had to go in the store to purchase my sanitary products. The women were so kind and sympathetic that they made sure to cover the top of the box with another paper bag. After I made my purchase, I then had the task of holding this big box while at the same time navigate riding a ten-speed bike for the fifteen-minute ride to my house. I prayed each time that I wouldn't run into any of my friends. This was a humiliating experience for me, and I vowed that I wouldn't do this to my daughter if I had one. I kept that vow!

* * *

"Danice, where is your coat?" one of my friends asked me.

I responded to her, "This is my coat. I want to wear my dad's fatigue jacket. This jacket is warm and comfortable." But the jacket really wasn't warm or comfortable. So, imagine a twelve-year-old girl in a grown man's jacket that was several sizes too big, with the sleeves rolled up and no hood. Then you will know that I felt every cold blast of winter air! Somehow, my mom neglected to get me a winter coat for school. It might have been her preoccupation with my three-year-old sister, who seemed to get all of the attention, clothes, and love from my parents. My baby sister, Renetta, seemed to have things that I lacked, like a good grade of hair that was longer than mine, a lighter complexion, and dimples. I wanted those dimples badder than I wanted anything! When Renetta smiled, it seemed like everyone zeroed in on those dimples. She had the deep kind of dimples that showed even when she talked. And you know a three-year-old talks a lot, so those dimples were on display like a piece of art at a museum.

* * *

"No Mama! I'll never do that again!" James Bentley screamed as his mother, Mrs.

Bentley, beat him with her leather belt in the principal's office. You could hear James' cries and screams throughout the whole elementary school. Mrs. Bentley was showing him no mercy since he acted up in class and the principal called her at home. Mrs. Bentley always walked to the school with her housecoat on, and her pink sponge rollers in her hair, carrying that thick, black leather belt in her hand. From our classroom, we could always see Mrs. Bentley coming up the sidewalk from her house. On this particular occasion, Lynnetta, Mrs. Bentley's daughter, was rocking in her desk beside me whispering, "Thank You God it's not me this time." Corporal punishment, or paddling as they called it, was allowed in the classrooms when I was in school back in the day. Either the teacher administered the paddling, or in severe cases, the principal meted out the punishment. James' cries still echoed throughout the school even after Mrs. Bentley had left the building.

Chapter 4: Let the Fun Begin!

I was a seventh grader and loving life! I had been back in my hometown of Myrtle Beach, SC, for the past ten months since my dad went to Korea for his year-long isolation tour. So Mom, Renetta, Terry, and I were back at Big Momma's house to wait out the year that my dad was out of the country. My grandfather, Big Daddy, had died while we were living in Oklahoma. So it was just Big Momma, my aunts/sisters, and my uncle/brother Robert in the house. My big brother Richard (Rich) had married and moved out of the house. We had to do some doubling up since there were ten people living in a four-bedroom house. My sister Rochelle and I slept on a roll-away bed in the den, while my mom and baby sister, Renetta, took up residence in her old room. Terry bunked in our brother/uncle Robert's room, and my other three sister/aunts— Rhonda, Ramona, and Rachel (yes, Big Momma had the "R" name theme going on)—shared a bedroom, while Big Momma had her own room. It was a tight fit, but we made it work.

* * *

"Go ahead and try it. It'll relax you and make you feel good," Johnny told me as he handed me the joint. I was thirteen years old and getting ready to take my first hit of reefer. I took a toke, inhaled the marijuana into my lungs, and started to cough. "Easy there! Don't pull so hard on the joint," Johnny admonished me. After I finished coughing, wiping my runny eyes, and drinking some soda, I tried the reefer again. This time, I didn't pull so long on the joint, and I had much better results. "That's it—now you got the hang of it!" Johnny cheered me on as I mastered smoking reefer. My first experience smoking marijuana with Johnny started a twenty-plus year tumultuous love affair with the drug.

* * *

"I made yearbook!" I shouted as I came through the front door. My mom stepped out of the kitchen where she was preparing dinner and congratulated me.

"Cool! What's yearbook?" my brother Terry asked as he stood at the entrance to the den. My baby sister, Renetta, was playing with a white baby doll on the floor, while the rest of my siblings were either working their part-time jobs or participating in extracurricular school activities. Big Momma was at work as a maid/nanny for a white family across town. "Yearbook is a group of students that take a bunch of pictures of things happening around school, then we put those pictures in a big book and sell copies to other students," I explained to Terry as simply as I could.

"Wow! I wanna run all over school taking pictures," he stated.

"We don't run around school taking pictures, silly. We go to certain events like basketball games, soccer games, and pep rallies. We take the pictures and save them to put in our yearbook," I explained.

"That still sounds like fun," Terry told me and our mom. I just laughed at him and went to the kitchen table to start on my homework.

* * *

"You all have been selected for this class because you are considered to be gifted and talented," Mrs. Schmidt told us one day in class. One of my classmates asked what "gifted and talented" meant, and Mrs. Schmidt explained that we tested high on the standards tests, so we were identified as being academically gifted and talented. I had never heard that term before, because at my old school in Oklahoma, we were just placed in different groups within the classroom according to our progress. I liked being "gifted and talented" because we went on special field trips, checked out more books from the library, and received other privileges that the other students in the school didn't get. Being the assistant editor on yearbook, getting special privileges in school, and my budding (pun intended) relationship with reefer had me on top of the world.

Chapter 5: Two Years Later

. . .

"Hey Danice! Come get in the car," my friend Vicky yelled from the driver's side of the car. I quickly left my place in the bus stop line and hopped into the back seat. Twin sisters, Anita and Benita, were already in the car with Vicky. My family and I were now living in Arizona because my father was stationed at Luke AFB, which is located just outside of Phoenix. As soon as we cleared the gates of the base, Anita sparked up a joint. We were getting our heads right before we hit the grounds of Dysart High School.

"This is so good," I said as I took a pull of the joint, letting the smoke fill my lungs. "This is that good stuff from Mexico," Benita told me as I passed the joint to her.

"Where did you get it from?" I asked no one in particular.

"I got this dime bag from Manuel in my physics class," Vicky told me as the reefer was passed to her.

"Well, you need to keep getting dime bags from him, because this right here is great!" I exclaimed from my back-seat position.

We arrived about fifteen minutes later at the campus of Dysart High School. The classrooms were housed in several buildings scattered across the campus. This set up was so different from what I was used to. I had gone to schools where all the classes and offices were in the same building. Here my walk to a class could be a long one, depending on what building I had to go to. My first class of the day was biology, and I couldn't deal with Mrs. Thompson's chipper butt so early in the morning. Especially on a day like today since I was high after catching a ride with Vicky. Anita, Benita, and Vicky were seniors, while I was the lone freshman of the group. All of our fathers were in the Air Force, and our parents met at the NCO Club at a brunch, so us kids by extension became friends, too.

* * *

I don't know why I let Vicky talk me into running track, I mumbled to myself as I was catching my breath. I had just run the second leg in the 4 x 100 relay race during our team's practice. I also did shot put and discus—two other events Vicky talked me into doing. After finishing practice, I was in the locker room changing when Toya approached saying she heard that I had been talking about her twin sister, Tonya. I finished dressing and faced her to fully understand what she was saying. "Why you got my sister's name in your mouth?" Toya ranted at me.

"Your sister's name is in everybody's mouth since she got pregnant by a nineteen-year-old," I sarcastically responded.

Next thing I knew, Toya was charging after me with arms flying. I started punching Toya in the face and stomach, getting in good blows until she latched onto my hair. Let me tell you that Toya's hair was about an inch long, styled in a Jheri Curl, whereas my hair was past my shoulders. "Get her hands outta my hair!" I yelled to no one in particular. There was a crowd of about ten girls surrounding us in the locker room, and no one moved. I yelled again for someone to get Toya's hands out of my hair, but to no avail. I managed to hit Toya in the stomach real hard so she would loosen her grip. After that, I started wailing on her butt again until Vicky and a few other girls broke us apart.

Toya stood there cussing at me while I looked at her calmly. Once we got outside, some of the girls started telling other members of the track team what had happened, and I got a crowd around me asking for details. After about ten minutes, we heard that Toya's big sister Lisa was coming. Obviously, someone (or Toya) called Lisa and told her that her baby sister was in a fight. Lisa came stomping up to me and said, "I heard you fought my sister Toya."

"Yes, and what about it?" I replied. Lisa was staring me down, and I returned the stare back with no fear in my eyes. Most people at school were afraid of Lisa because she was loud and liked to intimidate people. She was also gay, which was a no-no and shocker to us back in the mid-1980s. Lisa dated a big Mexican girl named Lupe, and they were terrors on our school campus. But Lisa didn't scare me because I grew up fighting girls and boys back home in Myrtle Beach.

As Lisa and I continued to stare each other down, Toya snuck up from the left and sucker punched me in the eye. That heifer! But I couldn't take my eyes off of Lisa because she was known to carry a knife, and I didn't know what she would do. "You good baby sis?" Lisa asked Toya, who nodded her head. Since Toya didn't get any hits in during the fight, she thought it was cool to sneak me since her big sis was there to back her up. Lisa, Toya, and their group walked off after this incident, and I'm left to catch a ride home with Vicky.

So now I had to sport a black eye for the next few days, with classmates and others coming up to me and asking me what happened like they were news reporters. One outcome was that Toya got suspended from school for five days, while I, the honor student, was able to still go to class. The other outcome was that I found out Vicky and a few girls from the track team told Toya that I was the one who was talking about her twin. They forgot to mention that they were talking about Tonya, too! After that revelation, I didn't hang with Vicky, Anita, and Benita or the other senior girls for months. That was a big betrayal that I couldn't get over for a while. Vicky and company thought that since I was quiet, a freshman, and not from there, I couldn't fight. Well, I showed all of them wrong because this Little Black Girl from Myrtle Beach could fight!

Chapter 6: Two More Years Later . . .

It's good to be back home! I thought to myself as I walked the halls of Myrtle Beach High School. After three years of living in Phoenix, I was glad to be back on the East Coast where the people were friendly and there was a beach within walking distance. It was good to be back with childhood friends, and also my boyfriend, Joey, who I was forced to lcavc when my family moved to Arizona. Things were different now because we are teenagers, and Joey was a gifted basketball player with scholarship offers from several major universities. Being a senior, Joey was focused on getting the best scholarship offer, whereas I was a junior with partying on my mind. But Joey and I found time to be together despite our busy lives.

"Come on Neesy! We've known each other for years," Joey murmured as he kissed my neck.

"You're right Joey. We have known each other for years. Plus, I'm on the pill. Do you have a rubber?" I said all of this in a rush since I was nervous as all get out about being intimate with Joey for the first time. I was so glad that I had been on the pill for about three months, because I could've predicted Joey and I were going down this road.

My mom had been lecturing me for years with her, "When you turn sixteen or your junior year in high school, whichever comes first, you are getting on the pill" speeches. Of course, I turned sixteen my junior year in high school, and Mom promptly made OB/GYN appointments for me and her four sisters. We all went to the hospital at Myrtle Beach AFB to get pap smears and birth control pills. How embarrassing is it to have your mother stand in the corner of the exam room with her arms folded across her chest, looking over the doctor's shoulder as you get your first pap smear?! I still cringe when I think of that day!

"Are you ok?" Joey asked after we finish our first-time having sex.

I nodded yes and then asked him to get me a drink. We were at a popular hotel where a lot of high school students used to have sex or just hang out without parental supervision or interference. Joey came back and handed me a beer, which I gulped down greedily. He then proceeded to light up a joint, which I was happy to smoke. After we finish drinking and smoking together, we took a couple's shower in the hotel bathroom. We still had a couple of hours before I had to be home to make curfew, so we drank some more beers and smoked another joint. Joey dropped me off at home on time with a sweet good night kiss and drove to his house fifteen minutes away. This was a night I didn't want to forget, so I was ready to fall asleep and relive this special night in my dreams.

Chapter 7: If You Can't Run with the Big Dawgs . . .

I was a freshman at the University of Georgia and loving it! College life was all I had heard about and more. The fine men, the parties, the nonexistent curfew, and the freedom. Did I mention the fine men? Men on UGA's campus represented every spectrum of the color scheme, from dark as midnight to light, bright dang-near white. These men were athletes, frat members, or regular Joes, but they were intelligent men with their futures mapped out and success on their minds.

I lived in Creswell Hall, aka "The Well," on the third floor. This was a coed dorm, with the guys living on the second floor. I chose this dorm because I couldn't see myself living in a place full of women. The Well had the misfortune of not having air conditioning, so a fan was a must. The running joke was that engineers from Georgia Tech designed the dorm, so they wanted UGA students to suffer.

"Hey Neesy! I got a guy for you to meet," my loud roommate announced. It was 2 o'clock in the morning, and this heifer

Leslie came into our room with two guys. I was in a deep sleep, so I was not happy to be woken up so late. I turned my head, which was covered in a red scarf, to the intruders, and I let the cuss words fly. I cussed them out so bad that the guys left our room, and one of them came back to apologize for disturbing my sleep. Once Leslie came back from walking them downstairs, we immediately got into an argument. We were so loud that a couple of girls from the floor knocked on our door to see if everything was alright. I told them I was sorry for the disturbance, but this needed to be done. Leslie and I argued every night around the same time for a week until the "Klan incident."

"One day, when you're walking back from work, the library, or class at night, I'll just have my Klan friends jump you," Leslie declared heatedly during one of our fights.

"Heifer, there goes the phone—dial!" I yelled back pissed and shocked. Leslie didn't make a move to the phone. Instead, she gathered up some clothes and left the room. The next day, I told a few sistas about the incident, and we set up a vigil on the elevators from the lounge area. For five hours we waited for Leslie, but she never showed up. In fact, Leslie stayed away from our floor for three days. I told the resident assistant (RA) and the graduate assistant (GA) about the incident, and the only thing they advised me to do was move out of the room. You have to remember that this was the late 1980s, and hate crimes or racist threats weren't on the radar then. Melissa, who lived up the hall from me, offered to let me move in with her since she didn't have a roommate. I happily packed up my stuff and moved up the hall.

Drink Until You Crawl was the theme for our hall's "Crawl Party." It was Halloween, and our hall put on a party. Each person paid $2, and they could drink however much they wanted from any of the rooms offering drinks. We had fuzzy navels, slow gin fizzes, rum and cokes—you name it, and we had it. Melissa and I served strawberry daiquiris. We added a twist and served popcorn from our air popper. We blasted Cameo's songs from their *Word Up!* album. You could hear *Word Up!* and *Candy* booming from our room as we served up daiquiris and popcorn. Our drinks were so good that we had a crowd in the room and a line out the door. I was a professional when it came to making daiquiris. I used pink lemonade, frozen strawberries, ice, and lots of rum (the premade mixes weren't invented yet). I sniffed the air, and the smell of marijuana was strong. "Somebody is smoking reefer," I told Melissa as we continued serving people.

Next thing we knew, someone yelled out, "Campus police!" and the crowd started scattering. People grabbed their drinks to go, and we hurriedly shut down production. Music off. Lights off. Door locked. There were ten of us in the tiny dorm room that Melissa and I shared as we listened to campus police walk down the hall, knocking on various doors. We don't even move when they knocked on our door. Once campus police left the hall, our remaining guests got one last drink and went back to their respective dorm rooms. Our hall made $120 from that party. A good time was had by all!

* * *

I stood in the circle of ten as Juan asked, "You too?" to the group. All of us were on academic probation from not doing so well in the fall quarter.

"My parents are gonna kill me!" exclaimed Yvette.

"I can't flunk out—I was an honor graduate!" David moaned as he put his head in his hands.

"I can't afford to flunk out of college. I have scholarships to keep!" was my comment to the group. We were all freshmen who graduated number ten or higher from our respective high schools. We had all met the previous summer when we were rising high school seniors. UGA had a four-day program where "the best and the brightest" high school students from around the country stayed on campus and went to classes to experience college life. This was also a big recruiting tool for the university.

Our group of ten Black students met, clicked, stayed in touch with each other over the year, and decided to attend UGA. "What are we going to do?" Juan asked the group.

"I'm getting ready to hit the library and bring my grades up," I responded.

"No more frat or sorority parties for me!" Debra exclaimed as she patted her chest.

"Neesy, I'm going with you to the library," Tonya replied.

"Me too!" came from Yolanda. We all discussed our various plans to study differently, not go to every campus party, and get off of academic probation by the end of the spring quarter. Tonya, Yolanda, and I hit the library diligently, and it paid off when I made the dean's list in the spring quarter!

It was the beginning of June, and I was finishing up my final exams. Two of my cousins were coming down from Atlanta to help me pack up my room and take my stuff to their apartment so I could fly out to Phoenix and retrieve my car from my parents' house. Sitting in first-class on the Delta flight from Atlanta to Phoenix was bliss! The drinks kept coming, and I was sitting between two rich and successful white businessmen. Their conversation was fascinating. Being the head of a multimillion-dollar company didn't seem to faze them—they took it all in stride. They encouraged me to finish college and to be successful in what I pursued. I appreciated that encouragement and confidence in my abilities.

Chapter 8: A New Beginning

. . .

"You did what?!" my mom yelled through the phone.

"I got married to Wayne two days ago," I repeated to her. The date was July 14th and Wayne and I got married on July 12th. A friend and coworker of Wayne's married us in his home with his three daughters looking on. We were both in shorts, and it was very casual.

"Now, you're getting ready to throw your life away. You're gonna end up pregnant and not finish college," my mom responded. I shook my head as a lump formed in my throat because of my mom's harsh words.

"No, I won't," I shoot back. "Wayne is very supportive of me finishing school, and we haven't even talked about having kids."

"Well, I'm gonna tell your daddy about this, and he's not gonna be happy," was my mom's quick reply.

It had been about three or four months, and I hadn't heard a word from my parents since my mom and I had that heated conversation about me being married. They were disappointed that I got married before my senior year of college and thought that marriage (to anybody) would derail my dreams. I was deeply hurt by their refusal to talk to me, but Big Momma helped to smooth things out. Big Momma told my mom how I was still in college and that Wayne was a good husband to me. My parents were also upset that I had left UGA and transferred to the University of South Carolina. I wasn't happy about going to Carolina, but it was the half-way point between Myrtle Beach and Athens. Wayne had transferred with South Carolina Department of Transportation from the Conway office to the Columbia office some months ago, so he was already settled when we got married.

It was my birthday, and I couldn't wait until Wayne got home. I had already cooked some steaks, baked potatoes, and made a salad. I was wearing some sexy lingerie and had Ready For The World's song *Love You Down* in the cassette player. This was our song, and I played it whenever we were having a romantic night, or I wanted some. Wayne came through the door with a gift-wrapped box in his hands. "Happy birthday,

Neesy!" he exclaimed as he gave me the box.

"Thank you dear," I replied as I grabbed the box and eagerly opened it. Inside the package was a pair of jeans that were too big and a pink sweatshirt. My face fell at what I revealed.

"You don't like them?" Wayne asked me as he looked at my face.

"Dear, I wanted that red Liz Claiborne drawstring purse I told you about a couple of months ago," I whined. "I even told you how much it cost and what store to get it from." I looked at the clothes with disgust.

"Since you don't like the outfit, I'll take it back and go get you the purse," Wayne stated. I smiled because I was the type of person who told you if I didn't like a gift. Plus, I didn't want to waste his money by not wearing a gift I didn't like. After the first couple of years of marriage, Wayne started to just give me money so I could buy the presents that I wanted. It was a win-win for both of us!

* * *

"What am I going to do?" I asked myself as I stared at the positive result on the pregnancy test. I just found out I was pregnant, and I was due to start graduate school in a month. I had finished my BS degree in biology the year before, and I decided to take a year off before starting grad school. Wayne had been hounding me for the last few months about starting a family, but I thought it was too soon since we had only been married for two years. So this surprise was not expected or wanted. Wayne came home from work, and I waited until after dinner to give him the news.

"How are you feeling, dear?" I asked Wayne after telling him about the baby.

"I'm excited as all get out!" Wayne exclaimed as he jumped out of his seat. "You know I've been wanting my own child to raise, so I can prove that I'm a better dad than my father was to me," Wayne stated firmly. Wayne and his father are estranged, and since his dad abandoned the family when Wayne was an infant, he didn't have a steady father figure in his life. So being a father was important to Wayne because he wanted to be active and present in his child's life. I let out the breath I was holding because saying you want a child and having a child are two different realities. I was relieved that Wayne was happy about the baby, even though it wasn't planned.

* * *

Grad school was hard. Raising a baby was hard. I was in my last semester of grad school, and I would receive a Master of Public Health in Public Health Administration in a few months. Rocking a baby, working part-time at an auto parts store, being a wife, and going to school was difficult, but I knew things would be better in a little while. Marceya, or Cee Cee for short, would be a year old in a few months. She was already walking and saying a few words like "Ma Ma," "Da Da," "stop," and her favorite word, "no." It was a joy watching my precious daughter. I found an older white woman in the neighborhood, Ms. Alice, who watched Cee Cee for $50 a week. That was a lot of money for Wayne and me to pay, since he made about $5 an hour at his state job, and I made $3.85 an hour at my job. My check covered childcare, while Wayne's check paid the rest of the bills. Thank God we didn't have a car payment, or I don't know how we would have survived.

"You going out again?" Wayne asked as I put on my earrings.

"Yes, I'm going out with Debra to Fountain Bleu," I responded.

"This is the second time this week you're going out," Wayne complained.

"It's ladies' night, and we get in free. Plus, we're sneaking in mini bottles of liquor, so we'll only have to pay for a soda," I calmly told him. Wayne rolled his eyes and walked out of our bedroom. I had developed party fever and loved going out to the local clubs in Columbia, SC, to have a good time. I would normally meet up with Debra at her house so we could have our own "Happy Hour" before hitting the club. "Happy Hour" consisted of us drinking and smoking reefer before heading out for a night of fun. And if we were lucky enough, Debra would see one of her male friends at the club who would hook us up with a free joint.

The club was packed! It was wall-to-wall people in Fountain Bleu. I knew the club was over its occupancy level, but it seemed like the owners didn't care if the fire marshal came through and shut it down. Debra and I made it through security with no problem. Our mini bottles of rum were safe since the security guard didn't look thoroughly in our purses once he saw the tampons as soon as we opened them. When a guy sees feminine products, it's like he's seen a snake and wants to run. We made our way to the bar and ordered our cokes. We then went to the bathroom where we poured out most of the Coke to make room for the rum. Then we mingled in the crowd, ready to get our party on.

"Are you married?" asked the guy with the beautiful smile.

"Yes, I am," was my reply.

"But are you happily married?" came his next question.

"Yes, I am" was my response as I flashed my wedding rings in his face.

"You look too good to be out here by yourself," Colgate smile shot back. I called him Colgate smile because of his nice, straight, white teeth. "You must not be too happily married if you came out here without your husband."

"My marriage is fine. I'm fine," I answered with bold confidence to his comment. It would be years later before I realized that my going out was a result of not being happy with myself or my marriage.

Chapter 9: Four Years Later

• • •

I'm back in Phoenix, AZ, but now I'm an adult instead of a teen. I have been back here for about a year. The move to Phoenix started with a phone call I received from my mom. "Neesy, are you ready?" came from Renee, my mom.

"Ready for what?" I replied back to her.

"Are you ready for your dad to come and move you to Phoenix?" was my mom's response.

"No. What made you think I wanted to move to Phoenix?" was my puzzling question.

"You told me that if you didn't find a job three months after you finished grad school, then you were moving to Phoenix," my mom calmly replied.

"I really didn't mean that Mom," I told Renee.

"Well I'm so glad your daddy didn't reserve that U-Haul," my mom told me in a huff. "Y'all might as well move to Phoenix because the job opportunities are way better here than in South Carolina," she stated as a matter of fact. "You can get a job with no problem in public health out here, and Wayne can get one with the highway department and do what he's doing in SC."

Renee told me as if I was slow on the uptake. "Mom, let me talk to Wayne and see what he says. You are talking about us moving across the country to a place he's only visited," I reminded her. I talked to Wayne later on that night, and we were on our way to Phoenix two months later!

***

"If y'all don't quit rubbernecking at that wreck on the other side of the road, I'm gonna be late for work!" I yelled as I sat in traffic on I-17 in Phoenix. It was 7:30 in the morning, and I had to be at work at 8. I had a horrible supervisor, Katie, who took pleasure in making her subordinates suffer. She made one girl fill out a leave slip for being two minutes late! I worked at the Department of Economic Security (DES) processing applications for the food stamp program. Traffic started to move, and I was on my way to the west side of Phoenix where my office was located. "I made it with two minutes to spare," I declared as I punched my time sheet. I wouldn't have been able to deal with Katie if I were late today. She already had it in for me since she found out I had a college degree and thought I wanted her job. NOT! Working food stamp cases and being in the human services field was not what I wanted to be when I grew up. I greeted my coworkers as I made my way to my cubicle. Being in "cube city" was not how I wanted a career either. I dreamed of being in my own office, doing what I went to school for—public health. I had been applying for jobs to get me closer to my goal, but no luck yet.

"Neesy, turn that up!" Ronesha yelled from a cube near me. Joe's *All the Things (Your Man Won't Do)* played on my radio. I cranked up the volume and could hear Ronesha and others singing along with Joe. I went through the cases on my desk so I could call my next applicant. In walked a girl with a two-year-old on her hip. "Sally" sat down, and we started the interview process for her food stamp recertification. As things went along, I found out that we were both twenty-seven, but that's where we stopped having things in common. Sally had four kids by four different men and was a third-generation welfare recipient. She told me that her mother told her to get pregnant and let the government take care of her. My mouth hung open as I listened to her story.

Sally had her first child at sixteen, then moved into her own Section-8 apartment at eighteen. By the time of her interview, she lived in a Section-8 house where she paid $50 a month for rent and received $175 a month per child in welfare so she could pay bills, buy food, etc. My client told me that her mom never pushed education, safe sex, or working to have good things. I was shocked that Sally was sitting in my cube and telling me how she was taught morals and values that led to a lifetime of poverty and dependence on someone else to take care of her. I felt bad about how my client's life turned out, but at the same time I was grateful that my parents preached getting an education, then getting a good job so I could support myself. I renewed Sally's food stamps, then escorted her up front so I could see my next client.

* * *

"Where are we going for lunch?" I asked Ronesha and Michelle while we were on our scheduled morning break.

"The usual place. I don't know why you even asked," came from Michelle. It was

Friday and payday, so the three of us always went to the Mexican restaurant down the street from the job. We were such regulars that the waiter would bring our drinks to the table once we sat down. Ronesha and I drank margaritas, while Michelle drank daiquiris. On some Fridays, we had a straight liquid lunch because of the stress of our jobs. Having to see eight applicants or more in a day would drive anyone to drink! Top it off with a supervisor from hell, and you would want to drink all day!

* * *

"What are you doing?" my supervisor Katie asked frantically as I was putting my personal items in a box.

"What does it look like I'm doing? I'm leaving this rat hole with your micromanaging behind." I calmly told Katie as I continued to put my snacks into the box.

"But you can't leave!" Katie cried out.

"Oh yes I can, because I got a better paying job with a nice supervisor who won't ride my butt for being a minute late or giving me crazy looks when I question her decisions," I snapped back. I was so happy to be leaving DES and heading to the Arizona Department of Health Services, or

ADHS for short. I was finally getting ready to put my Master of Public Health degree to work at the state health department.

"I am so happy and grateful to be working here," I told my department head, Scott. He and the division director, Patrick, were so good to me. Those two, along with another colleague named Mark, treated me like one of their kids. Whatever trainings I wanted to attend, they would let me go, and Mark was taking me all around the state to meet the constituents that we helped to bring much needed medical professionals to underserved areas of the state. There wasn't a town that we went to in the State of Arizona where Mark didn't know someone. When he retired a few years later, over two hundred people came to his retirement party, which included two nuns who rode over three hours to bring him fresh-baked bread!

* * *

"You mean I can get paid way more than I'm making now, receive military benefits, and still work in public health?" I asked José who was the Public Health Advisor assigned to our office from the federal government to assist us in streamlining our programs.

"Yes, Danice, you can get all that and more as part of the U.S. Public Health Service's Commissioned Corps," José replied. I couldn't believe what I was hearing—make more money, get a military ID again, and pursue my career in public health. Sign me up! I couldn't fill the application out for USPHS quick enough!

"Send me your resume, and I'll get you a job," the confident woman told me while we were in the bathroom applying our lipstick in the mirror. She had on a crisp white uniform with four bars on her shoulders.

Yea how often had I heard that before, I thought to myself as I continued grooming. In the past people had told me that they could get me a job, but nothing ever came of it. So I was skeptical when this woman said that she could get me a job.

"As soon as I get back to Phoenix, I'll send you my resume. Thank you for your help," I told the woman as we exited the bathroom. I was in Washington, DC, for the annual public health symposium between the state public health professionals and our federal counterparts to discuss various issues affecting underserved populations. I left a few days later with a business card that changed my life significantly!

Chapter 10: Moving On Up!

"We're moving to Maryland next month!" I shouted to Wayne over the phone. I had finished three interviews that day which resulted in a job offer to work at Health Resources and Services Administration (HRSA) as a policy analyst. I had come to Maryland the day before to prepare for my interviews. Helen, the woman I had met in the bathroom a month ago, came through on her promise to get me a job. Within a week of sending her my resume, I started receiving phone calls to set up interviews. I was able to arrange all three interviews for the same day since I was coming from Arizona.

"I'm so happy for you babe! I'm so proud of you!" Wayne exclaimed over the phone.

"I'm on my way to look at some apartments," I told Wayne. My soon-to-be new supervisor sent me to an apartment locator service that did the apartment researching for me. So I went and looked at apartments while I was in town.

* * *

"We hate to see you go, Danice, but getting a commission in the U.S. Public Health Service (USPHS) and the opportunity to work at the federal level is something you can't pass up," Patrick told me as we ate lunch at the Italian restaurant my office took me to for my going away party.

"I can't thank you and Scott enough for the wonderful opportunity you gave me to work in public health." I told Patrick sincerely.

"I've learned so much from all of you and about how important it is for everyone to have access to a medical professional, no matter where they live," I told the group of my colleagues. Our little group of twelve was like an extended family, and we had grown close over the years I worked at ADHS. I was sad to leave them, but excited for my new journey in Maryland to begin!

* * *

"This is your office, Lieutenant Harris," my supervisor, Linda, told me. "And we literally had to create your office from a closet." Linda laughed as she ushered me into my new digs. The only give away that this wasn't a "real" office was the lack of a window like the other offices. But I was happy for the large space and that I was finally out of cube city!

"Thank you again, Linda, for the opportunity and the warm welcome from you and my other colleagues," I sincerely told her.

"I'll give you some time to settle in, and please let the secretary know if you need additional supplies," Linda said as she was leaving my office.

This is a dream come true! I thought to myself as I settled into my new office, career, and life in Maryland. Getting used to wearing a uniform every day took some time, but there is no thought to it now. I just make sure that they are dry cleaned, pressed, and ready to go. My assignment in the bureau's policy office was a great accomplishment because not many Blacks get into policy, Helen told me one time when we went to lunch. This was evident, because out of a staff of twenty, only three Blacks worked on policy issues; one colleague was the computer tech and another was the secretary.

* * *

"You'll have to eat your lunch in my car because we just got called to meet with Senator Burns on the Hill," Linda told me when she entered my office. I hurried up and put on my service dress blue (SDB) jacket and grabbed my lunch. This was not the first time our office had a last-minute meeting on Capitol Hill with a senator or one of their staffers, because our bureau had several public health programs up for reauthorization.

"What program are we discussing with the senator today?" I asked Linda as she navigated the streets of DC.

"We will be talking about rural health clinics and why Congress needs to reauthorize them for ten more years," Linda replied. Senator Burns was sponsoring this reauthorization bill, and our office met with him frequently to go over important benefits of rural health clinics so he could have talking points for his discussions with colleagues.

"Y'all help yourselves to something to eat," Senator Burns invited us as we came into the conference room. There were about three long tables full of all types of food including various kinds of sandwiches, salads, pasta dishes, and a whole table full of decadent desserts from cookies to tiramisu. If I had known we were going to the Hill, I would've saved the ten dollars I spent on lunch to eat this delicious spread that my tax dollars paid for. There are only about twelve of us here, so all of this food would go to waste—our government dollars at work in a not so good way.

"Danice, you'll probably only recognize one or two of your sentences once you get your document back," John warned me as we sat in the meeting and discussed the policy I would be drafting. John was a bureau director, and his bureau handled rural health care issues. I had written a three-page document, and sure enough, by the time the big wigs got through dissecting it and adding their own words, I only recognized two of my original sentences from the draft! This was the life I lived drafting Federal Register Notices, health care access policies, and serving underserved populations documents. I enjoyed seeing how all the pieces fit together before they went down to the state level. There were so many layers to developing and then implementing a policy from the federal government!

Chapter 11: Four More Years Later . . .

"Girl, I hate my job!" I told Mary in a low harsh tone.

"Neesy! You've got to be kidding me," Mary looked at me in horror. "You come in here every day smiling, greeting everyone, and you do the same thing on your way out of the office." Mary's shocked expression was still on her face.

"You nor anyone else in this office shouldn't have a clue that I can't stand my job. I'm supposed to come in with a smile on my face like I love my job," I responded.

"Neesy, you come in here every day looking like a million bucks. Uniform all pressed and sharp. Gucci on your wrists, and you telling me that you hate your job?" Mary asked.

"Yes, ma'am. I hate this job with a passion," was my reply.

I had been working for the Food and Drug Administration (FDA) for three years now. I was a Senior Program Management Officer, or project manager according to my supervisor, Patty. I interacted with pharmaceutical companies and individual investigators as they worked on clinical trials, protocols, etc. before they put in their new drug application (NDA) or investigational new drug (IND) application. But I considered myself a glorified secretary because I set up team meetings, typed up meeting notes, communicated with pharmaceutical managers, and kept the review team on track with milestones, deadlines, etc. I got paid very well for what I did (low 100s), but the job wasn't challenging. This job had a never-ending to-do list, which I never could seem to finish. Dealing with companies like Eli Lily, Johnson & Johnson, Glaxo-Smith-Kline, and smaller biopharma companies always kept me busy. I see why most project managers burned out after two years because of the stressfulness of the work. I was still there after three years, so something must have been wrong with me.

"Neesy, I think you need to see someone," Wayne told me one evening after I got in from work. "Cee Cee and I have to look at your face as you're walking to the front door to try to figure out what kind of mood you're in," he continued. "This has been going on for months. Plus, you've been complaining of all-day headaches for a while, so you need to get those checked out, too." I just sat there in shock as Wayne told me how I was unconsciously acting toward my family and that I needed some kind of mental help.

* * *

"This plantation is slowly killing me," I told the psychiatrist I had been seeing for the past two months.

"So you see your job as a plantation?" Dr. Carter asked.

"Yes. FDA is very racist. People who look like you and me don't go to certain meetings. We do the work of writing talking points, discussion papers, or white papers, and get no recognition. Massa want to use us for the skills we have, but parade the White interns around like they're the best things since sliced bread," I told Dr. Carter with a sad tone and expression on my face. I went on to explain, "I'm not the only Black person at FDA who calls the agency the plantation." The stress of the plantation and life had brought me to the point to where I was seeing a shrink weekly to talk about my life. This was not good!

* * *

"Commander, you have been diagnosed with migraine headaches. Based on your food diary, certain foods, drinks, and spices trigger your migraines, along with stress." This came from Dr. Higgins, my neurologist. I sat there with relief running through me. At least I didn't have a brain tumor or some sort of cancer. Migraines—I could live with them. Take some pills, watch what I eat and drink, and try to de-stress. But this was easier said than done! "Commander, you'll need to take migraine medicine daily for the rest of your life. I'll also prescribe you medicine to take at the onset of a migraine," Dr. Higgins went on to inform me. Not only was I taking meds for depression (did I forget to mention that?), but I also now had migraine meds added to my list. This was the first time in my life that I had to take medicine daily to manage what are called chronic health conditions.

* * *

"I can't take these drugs no more! My appetite is jacked up (even though I lost twelve pounds), and my sex life is in the toilet!" I exclaimed to my primary care doc.

"Commander Harris, we can take you off of the depression meds and put you on something else, but you can't stop taking the migraine meds," Dr. Jones replied to my outburst.

"I don't want to take any meds for my depression. I feel like a zombie, and I don't even want my husband to touch me, which isn't natural," I complained. "I'm in my early thirties and enjoyed a frequent and satisfying sex life until these drugs came into my life."

"Ok, Commander, we'll stop the Wellbutrin for now, and revisit this in a couple of months," Dr. Jones replied. I think Dr. Jones agreed with me because he saw how agitated and upset I was over these drug side effects.

Chapter 12: Outta Control!

"Light it up. Blow it out like a candle," I mimicked the lines to Eric B. and Rakim's *Know You Got Soul* classic rap song as I lit up the blunt I had just rolled. It was the weekend, and Wayne and I were chilling in the basement smoking reefer and watching DVD movies. Even though I was in the military, I hadn't stop my marijuana smoking. In fact my smoking had increased since I joined the military because I could afford it and I had steady access to it. Wayne and I smoked daily, and we were such good customers that our dealers would make home deliveries. I was spending 2k a month on weed and didn't miss it. Spending that much for reefer was like buying a Gucci handbag—a needed necessity!

* * *

"Commander Harris, you will report to National Naval Medical Center (also known as Bethesda Naval) in two weeks for your yearly physical," my supervisor, Patty, told me as she handed me a letter. I thanked Patty and looked over the letter once she left my office. Even though this physical was nothing new, I was apprehensive about it for some reason. The physical always included a urine analysis (UA), and I had aced it with no problem. One of my dealers told me about a product at GNC that would clear my system out in twenty-four hours. I made a pit-stop at GNC on my way home from the plantation so I could be prepared to pass my physical in a couple of weeks!

* * *

"I don't feel good," I told my colleague Mary as we ate lunch in the employee break room.

"What's wrong with you Neesy?" Mary asked me with a look of concern on her face.

"I don't know. My stomach's been churning all week, and that's not a migraine," I replied. I had to report to Bethesda Naval in four days for my physical. I had stopped smoking reefer, and I had taken the system cleaning product that morning. I just had an overall feeling of malaise all week. Something heavy was pressing on me, but I couldn't shake it, nor did I know what caused it. "I'll be glad when this physical is over," I said as I nibbled on my salad. My life would go back to normal after Thursday—I could smoke my weed again and enjoy life. Little did I know that my life wouldn't go back to normal in seven days!

* * *

"Go Neesy! It's your birthday!" I cheered as I danced around the room paraphrasing 50 Cent's *In Da Club* hit song. The date was September 25th, and I had four more days until my birthday, so I was doing a little pre-birthday celebrating with a glass of Courvoisier and coke and a blunt. Wayne was dancing with me as I continued to sing along with the song.

"Drop it low, Neesy," Wayne crooned in my ear as I grinded on him with my back facing his front. I dipped low, straightened my legs where my butt was in Wayne's crotch, and started to work it.

"Now that's what I'm talking about!" Wayne shouted as he smacked my butt. It takes skill to hold a glass of liquor in one hand and a blunt in the other while shaking your butt. Let's just say that I got skills!

Epilogue

After my near-death experience on my dining room floor the night of my pre-birthday celebration, I called my mom to tell her what happened. She started to cry during my story. And after the tears stopped, she gave me some Bible verses to read including the go-to of Bible chapters—Psalm 23—which I read over and over. Renee also gave me Proverbs 4 and John 3:16: "For God so loved the world that He gave His only begotten Son, that whoever believes in Him should not perish but have everlasting life" (NKJV). Reading these verses brought back to my mind all the years I had gone to Sunday school and church through my freshman year in high school, then church only my last two years of high school. I clearly remembered the few times I didn't go to Sunday school or church—I had the mumps on one occasion and the chicken pox on another.

Having read those Bible verses over and over from the time my mom gave them to me throughout the month I was out of work, I was open spiritually to an encounter with God. And that's what happened in that hotel room in Clemson, SC. God called me, and I answered Him by giving my life to Jesus Christ. That Bible verse is so true:

Train up a child in the way he should go, And when he is old he will not depart from it. (Proverbs 22:6, NKJV).

I was trained up in the church, departed from it when I went to college, and returned back to the church as an older adult. Jesus was always knocking at the door of my heart all those years, patiently waiting for me to open it and let Him in. I'm so glad Jesus waited!

I also didn't realize that my pre-birthday celebration with Wayne would be my last time hitting a club—an actual one or one made in my home. It took me six months of straddling the fence with one foot in the world and one foot in the church before I decided to follow God whole heartedly. I immediately stopped smoking reefer after I almost died. But I struggled with cussing and being impatient at stores (I hated waiting in line for more than ten minutes).

It took a month to break my habit of cussing. I had Wayne, Cee Cee, and my colleagues slap my hand when I said a cuss word and say, "Bad word!" to me. Once when I was leaving a team meeting, my division director turned around, slapped my hand and said, "Bad word!" I was shocked because I had no idea he knew I was trying to stop cussing. I thanked him and went back to my office smiling. However, it took me more than a month to be patient and wait in line at the grocery store or department store.

My faith in God was growing each day. I became eager to read my Bible each night—it is the best true story I have ever read! Did I have moments of doubt about my salvation? Of course, I did! Did I have my pity parties where I cried about almost dying and leaving Wayne and Cee Cee? You bet I did! Did I have times where I was too tired to pray or read my Bible? I sure did! But I kept at it and asked God to guide me, to give me strength, and to keep me safe. And guess what? God did!

Regardless of my circumstances such as being molested as a child, set up by friends (not in a good way), frustrating jobs, depression, drug addiction, and self-esteem issues, I have been able to overcome these obstacles with the help of the One True God. Jesus told me that I am an overcomer despite the life I lived because I have kept my eyes on Him instead of my surroundings. It has been seven months since my encounter with God in the hotel room, and I've been busy! I joined a little church on the side of the road near my house. I was baptized in the Name of the Father, the Son, and the Holy Spirit. I started reading my Bible for fifteen minutes a day. But the most important thing is that I started praying to God every day! My life has turned around for the better, and I look forward to each new day that the Lord brings me!

This journey is not over . . . there will be a Part 2!